the warning

You know what you're walking into.

SO, I won't sugarcoat it.

Yes, there will be blood, screaming, degradation, objectification, drugging, forced gagging, kidnapping, captivity, blindfolds and bondage used in non-consensual contexts, golden showers, threats of murder, graphic violence, bidding for harm, gore references, gangbangs, recording/filming of sexual acts without consent, dubious consent, forced breeding, trafficking dynamics, voyeurism, Stockholm syndrome, and anything that could potentially happen when the camera starts rolling once the chatroom is locked.

Adult readers only.

This is a dark romance intended for those who want to experience a twisted love with pain and nightmares.

Don't say I didn't warn you.

pretty girl

A Dark Captive Erotic Novella

Katrina Yang

copyright

contents

00:00:00

[ANNIEWALKERS88]: Been waiting weeks
for this one. First cry on me — 10
[CRYBABY2345]: new girl's pretty. I'd
say the blindfold comes off — 22
[ANONYMOUSMEMBER10]: blindfold stays
on — 100
[ANONYMOUSMEMBER040]: 50 for red
[CRYBABY2345] 10 — gag off
[ANONYMOUSMEMBER10]: 101 for the gag
[CRYBABY2345]: 102 — the gag is mine…
[SYSTEM NOTICE]: COUNTDOWN BEGINS. 12
HOURS REMAINING.

…

00:13:26

I fought to open my eyes, but even though I was blinking, everything still looked dark.

My wrists strained against something thick and harsh.

Ropes.

I vaguely remembered trying to fight them off back in the van. Now, every tiny movement burned.

My arms and shoulders were numb.

They were pulled over my head.

My head felt woozy, and my legs were shaking.

I felt the wind against my skin. When I pressed my knees together, my thighs touched.

Where were my jeans?

Was I even wearing anything?

I wanted to check myself, but my eyes were covered by a blindfold.

I was hung in this room.

Possibly stripped.

The intentions of whoever was behind this became the only thing that mattered... and over and over again, I prayed that they weren't after my body parts.

A loud alarm soared through the air, sending a cry up my lungs. I clenched my teeth on the piece of cloth in my mouth as the sound pierced my eardrums.

My hands kept shaking in the ropes.

Fuck...

The light switched on.

Bright, fucking light.

I gasped and almost choked on the dirty, wet cloth.

I fought to open my eyes. I blinked hard, but my world remained dark underneath the blindfold.

I had never wanted something this bad in my life, and now that something was to see my surroundings.

But I was trapped in the dark.

Powerless.

Helpless.

A girl in ropes.

I heard footsteps echoing in the distance.

It sounded like someone stepping down the stairs. A loud, stiff thud each time.

Slow.

Taunting.

Heavy.

He stopped briefly at the end of the stairs, and I heard him moving toward my direction.

Steady.
But eager.
Smug.
Experienced.
Calculated.
Confident.

A loud clang when he sprang the door open, and there was a shift in the room.

My teeth clenched the cloth, not daring to make a single sound.

My heart was pounding, but all of me was focused on him, what he was doing, and what he intended to do.

The sound of machines started — some kind of fan being switched on.

I heard his breathing.

Slow and steady.

Much like his footsteps.

He put something heavy and metal-ish on a table. His fingers hit what sounded like a keyboard.

He chuckled, as if amused by something he saw.

And then, there was silence.

A gritty scrape of his boots dragged across the floor.

He turned around.

And the way he breathed changed.

I heard his spine crackle.

The next thing was his footsteps moving toward me.

Dread rained down on my head.

My heart raced.

My mouth felt dry.

My body was shaking, and even though I knew it was no use, I still tried to wiggle free from the knots.

He stopped right in front of me.

The next thing I felt was his knuckles brushing across my lower belly, moving up the side of my body.

"It feels like a crime to touch you, knowing this body has never been touched with desire," he whispered, his voice one of deep melancholia but soft. "But that's exactly what makes you perfect, isn't it?"

For what?

My heart skipped a beat.

There was rhythm in the way he talked. Something lush and dark in the way he touched me.

My screams turned into muffled cries. I sobbed and grunted like a pig. I didn't want to be touched, but all I could feel was the way his fingers lingered.

His hand moved up to my tit. I felt his knuckles drag along my ribs, then loosen as his grip opened, and the shape of me filled his hand.

For a second, it was just the heat of his skin against the coldness of mine.

Then pain soaked in as he clamped down on it, hard and possessive.

I gasped, feeling my chin caught in his other hand. And the way he breathed changed again as he took a moment to look at me.

"Oh, the things I'll do to you," he breathed against my mouth, his tone velvety and sinful. "Don't be afraid, love. I'm only going to stain you a little. You'll like it. You'll love it. By the end of the day, you'll beg me to do it again. Oh, I'm very, very good at turning good girls into something else."

I felt a tug on the cloth in my mouth, and the next second, my jaws were relieved.

He pulled the gag out, but before any noise could be made, he leaned in, tipped my chin toward him, and seized my lips with his. His tongue unlocked my teeth and Frenched me.

I meant to do something about it, but his presence swallowed me like a dark angel. I tasted his lust, his desire, his chaos and heartbreak — all-consuming and addictive... seductive but a little broken.

His hand moved to the back of my head, his fingers weaving through my hair, tightening his grip, pressing me to him. He was moaning softly and needily when he kissed me.

My nostrils picked up the scent of his cologne, light but expensive; his minty aftershave; the hint of cigarette and bubblegum; his lips, soft and lush.

His thumb brushed lovingly across my nipple as he held my breast. His grip tightened when he deepened the kiss, his body moving against mine like there was a turmoil inside him that wanted to come out. And every time his tongue tugged against mine, I felt my knees pull together.

I had never been kissed like this before — like he meant it, like he couldn't live without me.

It messed with my head a little because I didn't believe him, and yet a part of me wanted to.

I didn't kiss him back, but I didn't bite his tongue off

either. I just stood there in the darkness, letting him fold me into his presence.

But then... a sharp, biting pain landed on my left butt cheek, the slap loud enough to jolt my whole body forward.

I cried out and bit down on his tongue. He hummed in pleasure, nudging my teeth to open, then licked my mouth sweetly and lovingly, as if I'd given him exactly what he wanted.

He reached down to the area of impact, caressing it gently.

"Cute noise she made," he whispered, breathless and lost. "So hot."

He drew circles with his palm, adding a little pressure every time it moved down. He rubbed my cheek and squeezed it a little, playfully and teasingly, right on the line between an innocent touch of care and lusty exploration.

My heart would race, then ease.

His hand never slipped between my legs. He never went over the line, and yet, with each circle he drew with his palm, I thought about him crossing it.

I hated how dizzy I felt.

How badly I wanted to bite him again.

"The current bid for this piece of cloth is one hundred and two thousand euros," he mused. "I can verify that it has stayed in her mouth for more than twelve hours, and it is soaked, guys. As a friendly reminder, the bidding will only be finalized at 1100."

He leaned into me, and I felt him breathing against

my skin. "One-oh-two. Can you believe it?" he whispered to me. "This is how much someone will pay to own a little piece of fabric that has touched your lips—"

His thumb brushed against my cheek, and then I felt his touch leave me. My heart dipped with a sudden emptiness.

A second later, a hard strike landed on the same area.

I cried, pressing my knees together hard.

He gripped those cheeks, pushing them up, moaning into my ear.

"Only I get to taste you," he bit out the words. "You're mine, pretty girl."

His touch left me again, and then came the sound of his pants being unzipped. I felt his arm shaking behind me. Ragged noises spilled into my ear like a confession.

"Guess how many men are touching themselves in this instant, wishing they were in the same room with you," he said.

I bit my lips to keep them shut.

"A thousand, two hundred ninety-four," he whispered, the words like a spell.

A soft gasp escaped my chest.

He slid his hand down my curve, gripping my hips, bending me forward, and I felt something hot, thick, and heavy being placed on my butt cheek.

For a very brief second, my mind went blank.

All I could feel was a pulse on my tender place, soaked and wanting...

His hands clutched my cheeks, dragging me against him as he drew a sharp, shaky breath.

"You want it?" His voice sounded wet and a little shy.

My fingers tightened around the ropes.

My breath trembled on its way out.

"No... Please... don't do this to me..." I begged, but a moan came out.

The fans buzzed over my head.

All I could feel and think about was the way that hot, heavy thing pressed against my skin, how it felt both tender and hard.

My hips moved to his touch like it was a drug. Slick heat dripped down my thighs as I felt him wetting my skin with a similar desire.

He pulled away from me for a moment, and the absence of his heat made something in me twist.

The machines spilled out a queasy, droning hum. Then I heard him unbuckling his shirt, button by button, and every nerve in my body lit up.

His dripping tip brushed my lower back softly. I inched back a little, counting the number of buttons he had undone.

An ache rose in my body, deep in my bones — something I shouldn't want. Something I shouldn't have... not like this... not in here... not with him... until he threw his shirt aside, and I moaned as his heat drew closer to me.

"Stop..." I shut my legs all of a sudden. "You get away from me!" My wrists fought the ropes.

The scraping pain made all my other feelings go quiet for a moment, but still, my heart ached when I heard myself.

"You don't want me now?" His voice sounded wet and a little hurt.

His fingers curled at my violent shifts, feeling my struggles brush against his knuckles.

For a moment, he just stood there, like an abandoned child, letting that hot, thick thing stumble down my curve before an unfortunate shift slammed it onto a much more sensitive part of me.

He caught my hips, stopping me there.

My wrists pulsed hotly.

"Please don't hurt me..." I whimpered.

He picked up a strand of hair and tucked it behind my ear, caressing the side of my face.

"I can't promise that," he whispered, biting my earlobe softly, almost as if he were sad. "You know I can't, love."

A loud spank landed on my left cheek. My lower belly clenched helplessly.

Another one landed on the other, rough enough to make my nose sting.

He cupped the areas that felt so raw and squeezed them hard, lifting them, and I felt that hot, thick thing pushing to my soft core, slow and deep.

He growled shakily, pulling my cheeks in wild circles, and each time he parted them, that big thing would grind a bit deeper.

A lusty noise trembled through my parted lips. My eyes closed under the blindfold.

He pulled my cheeks together and pushed them up

and down on his erection as his lips folded around my earlobe lovingly.

"You like that?" he whispered.

I swallowed, my body hot and heavy.

"I want it deeper in you," he hushed. "So I can feel you. Deeper."

I murmured something inaudible, mesmerized by his words.

"Would you like to be mine, love?"

I nodded without thinking.

At that, his lips drew up into a curve against my ear.

A playful spank landed on my lower back.

He nudged me forward to adjust closer, pressing his forehead against the back of my head, bending me a bit more for him, and I felt him place that hard thing on my lower back.

A moment later, something wet and hot spilled out of it.

He grunted, pressing his forehead harder to me as the stream pooled down my curves and legs.

It took me a second to wrap my mind around what he was doing.

As soon as I did, my face started to burn.

I wanted to move away from him so badly, but he pinned me to his chest, holding me in his arms, not letting me go, and the way his lips pressed against my neck made it feel like marking me was the hottest thing in the world.

I hated it so much — not because I was covered in

pee, but because of how much I wanted to stay in this moment.

Just like this.

In his arms.

A little longer.

Tears slipped from the corners of my eyes, but the blindfold caught them before they fell.

It was so exhausting to hate him.

To pretend that I had to fight.

For whom?

Little by little, the fight I had left my body.

My face still burned, but no longer for the same reason.

He turned my face to him and kissed me after he was done, and this time, I kissed him back, sobbing into his mouth.

He wove his hand into my hair, pulling me closer to him, and pressed his forehead against mine.

"Shhh..." he hushed softly. "I'm here. I'm right here."

He placed his cock back to my sensitive place with affection, where it belonged, and he started to touch me — really touch me.

His fingers parted the soft lips of mine and pressed his thickness between them. Each thrust made my core curl.

He spanked me — so hard that my knees pulsed — but he gripped my cheek even harder and buried himself deeper in my opening.

I clutched the ropes, my legs shaking, my breath disrupted.

He wrapped his arm around me, his head pressed hard against mine, his thick heat inching in, and the space between us became wet and sweaty.

"Condom?" he asked, moving back and forth in a low, hungry motion.

His hand reached down to my lower belly, caressing the region.

"I guess not."

A noise escaped my lips as my belly clenched violently at the indication.

At that, he grunted, catching my cheek with his other hand, squeezing it tight to stop me from moving under him.

"Ah, shit..." he moaned. "Easy. You're gonna make me come too fast. Pretty girl, I still want to fuck you first."

Breathless gasps mumbled through my parted lips.

I felt like I could faint any second.

I strained against the ropes, biting down on my teeth, trying not to clutch so much, but his words made me pulse even harder; each felt like a wave crashing against my flooded core.

His fingers brushed across my ribs to my breast. He cupped the left one tenderly, his mouth seeking my shoulder, sucking my skin like a drunk man. At that, I felt his hips swing wider and faster.

"Fuck me..." he murmured against my skin, spilling desperate little sounds.

"Wait for me, love," he begged, thrusting in and out of me harder and louder. "Don't come yet..."

Slick heat dripped down my thighs.

I could taste my heartbeat on my tongue.

"I can't..."

A cry caught in my throat. A violent pulse ripped through my lower belly.

I tried to keep it in, but my body was trembling so much... I shook my head as tears wet my cheeks.

A sharp scream pierced through the air. I came — so intensely that my world went dark.

01:12:45

[CRYBABY2345]: did she just pass out?
[ANNIEWALKERS88]: don't stop — 88
[ANONYMOUSMEMBER10]: play with her. I
wanna see her come like this — 50
[CRYBABY2345]: cream pie - 20
[ANONYMOUSMEMBER040]: cum on tits - 40
[CRYBABY2345]: cream pie - 50
[ANONYMOUSMEMBER040]: in her mouth — 60

03:58:15

In my dream, he held me in his arms and released me from the hook that had been pulling my arms up. He carried me out of the filthy room to a different one — one that felt like his. He put me down. For the first time in a very long time, my back touched the softness of a bed, and a soft hum resonated in my body.

He draped a feathery blanket over me and tucked me in. Then he leaned in and pressed a kiss to my forehead. When he tried to pull back, he hesitated, his lips lingering. His breath suddenly turned hot and a little urgent, like that small touch had barely been enough.

He lowered his head and pressed his lips to mine, tipping my face toward him. Then he ripped the blanket off between us, pulled my knees up, and tucked them under his arms. He folded me as he kissed me longingly, like he was aching to taste me again... like he wasn't done with me.

I was far from done with him.

I tried to haul my eyes open. I wanted to kiss him back the same way he kissed me, to feel him the way he felt me — but I couldn't move.

My head felt so heavy.

My eyes wouldn't open.

I opened my eyes.

This time, darkness didn't return.

I was allowed to see the world as it was.

There was a throbbing pain in my head, like someone had hit me with a baseball bat. The world was twirling fast. My vision stayed blurry until the fog lifted.

He was here, lying next to me, staring at the ceiling with his arm stretched out. And I was sleeping on it, clutching him like a child.

He had tattoos on top of tattoos, scraped and redone. His lips were smeared red, and his face was painted a sickly pale. Black circled his eyes, making him look like a ghost.

"Had to give you something to make you sleep a bit longer," he murmured, curling his lips. "It helps with the pain, though."

He turned his head toward me. Those eyes he tried so hard to hide were exposed now. They were deep and tortured, like they suffered from feeling everything too intensely.

My heart raced. For a moment, I forgot how to breathe. All I could pull from my head was the way he fucked me in the dark.

"Were you hoping for someone prettier?" he said with a teasing grin, leaning in.

I instinctively shifted back.

"Don't move." He caught me by the shoulder, staring at my mouth. "You've got a bit of me on your face."

He lifted his hand, licked his thumb, and pressed it to the corner of my lips to wipe away the red. He sucked it off, and something flickered in his eyes.

He pulled me closer to him and guided my mouth to his. He opened me with his lips and claimed me.

My fingers gripped his arm without my permission. I was letting him, tasting him, with my heart pounding dangerously while my mind stayed stuck in the dark with him, replaying every touch, every thrust.

He watched me quietly, observing me, studying me, like he wanted to see exactly what was going on in my head as I tasted him.

And there, he smiled.

"Now you look like me," he said, rubbing my lower lip with his thumb to spread the color. "So pretty."

My fingers clutched his arm involuntarily.

What is this?

My heart drummed so hard in my chest. I swallowed and lowered my head to break away from his touch, but it lingered on my skin like a stain.

I was parting my lips, responding to him like I was addicted to it. To him.

I missed the blindfold. Because somehow, it had made everything feel so much safer.

This was dangerous...

He was dangerous.

My eyes landed on my wrists, swollen, red, and covered in cuts. I wasn't in bondage anymore. I guessed the broadcast was over — and yet I couldn't stop the flutters, the breathlessness, the way my whole body ached with this suffocating desire to be owned by him again.

"I sold the ropes," he whispered, leaning in, letting his breath spill over my earlobe. His lips drew up into a curve on my skin. "One hundred and two thousand euros. Not bad."

I swallowed, my heart pulsing to the rhythm of his words. This felt so unnatural, even more so than being stripped and hung on a hook.

He stretched his arms and dragged his laptop from the nightstand, placing it in front of me. He clicked on an icon, and a video popped up.

Moaning noises of a woman and a man filled my ears with filth. I looked away, but he reached for my chin and made me watch.

I recognized his moans in the video. It sounded a little different from how I remembered, but it still woke a monster in me. He was whispering in her ear as he fucked her, the same way he did me, and the woman in the video was clearly enjoying it.

I wanted to look away, but he didn't give me much of a choice.

"You recognize this?" he asked, propping his arm behind me, and I felt his skin brush my back.

I shook my head.

"It's you, pretty girl," he whispered in my ear, bruised and hungry, and the distance between us nearly disappeared. "You were so hot in a blindfold. God... I made you faint, coming that hard."

"I... came?" I gasped.

"I felt every bit of it," he hushed, biting his lip.

A shameful heat rose between my legs.

"I can prove it." He tapped on the laptop, and the footage changed.

It was no longer one screen but four, capturing the act from every angle.

The one he showed me first was the broad view, but there were three other feeds: one pointed at my pussy in a close shot, one fixated on my face, and another showing our bodies from up top.

Was that really how I looked on camera?

How I sounded?

Was my pussy really that wet, being stretched that wide to take his girth?

I couldn't help pressing my knees together again, and pain reminded me that I was still new to this.

He was watching me as I watched the video.

"There were more after you checked out," he said, his voice dark and alluring, as if sending me an invitation to a forbidden party. "You want to see it?"

My eyes were glued to the footage.

I was going to shake my head, but I nodded.

"Good girl." He grinned.

He dragged the locator all the way to the point when I had stopped moving and paused the video.

He patted his lap, gesturing for me to sit.

My eyes danced over his crotch. I bit my lips, wanting but afraid.

He chuckled softly, as if he had read my mind. Instead, he put his hands under my armpits, lifted me, and put me on his lap.

The familiar aroma of his cologne filled my world again. I felt his hands moving around the sides of my body as he started breathing in my ear, and I felt them edging the front.

A moan shivered through my lips as he seized my breasts, rubbing them together.

He let go of one and clicked to start the video, and the breathless noises spilled from the speaker again.

He slid under my shirt and grabbed my breasts again. My legs clutched.

In the video, he was panting behind me while my head dangled from my neck.

My eyes caught the bidding war happening in real time in the live chat, trying to decide what would happen to me next. My fingers curled into fists on my lap. My face turned hot.

I couldn't believe I was turned on by this. Moreover, I was... rooting for my own ruin.

Don't cut the camera.

Keep going.

Fill her cunt with cum.

"Make up your mind, mate," his hoarse voice came through the speaker and startled me a little. "I can't hold it much longer."

A few thrusts later, he halted.

"Fuck me..." He pulled his cock out and grunted, pressing his lips together as if trying to repress something.

No. Don't stop.

I almost cheered when he shoved it back into me. His hand reached down between my legs, and I watched him rub my clit in the small screen as his cock stuffed me like a little pound cake.

The live chat kept rolling. They fought over where he'd come.

He was a mess in the video. A few thrusts, then pull out, trembling. Shove it back in and pant. Until Annie-Walkers88 outbid everyone and placed two thousand euros on a cream pie to "save our boy."

And I watched his cock twitch so deep inside me as his fingers rubbed my pussy. A few seconds later, he pulled out. White cream leaked out as my little hole tightened and opened. A few drops dripped on the camera, blocking the sight.

Oh fuck...

Oh fuck...

I was shamefully squeezing my legs, not wanting him to notice that I'd soaked my panties again, while he caressed my lower belly, pressing something hard between my legs again.

I could still feel his marks on my pussy...

[CRYBABY2345]: dibs on the rope – 22
[ANONYMOUSMEMBER0818]: her virginity - 50
[ANONYMOUSMEMBER10]: 60 – her virginity
[ANONYMOUSMEMBER040]: 75 – her virginity
[ANNIEWALKERS88]: I want her after this is over -
 500

...

He swept the laptop aside while keeping the video rolling. His palm lingered around my lower belly, where he'd had it filled.

"Who got me in the end? AnnieWalkers88?" I moaned, melting like a hot, wet mess under his touch.

"Does it matter?" he whispered. His fingers tugged the edge of my shirt, pulling it over my head, and his hands returned to my tits again, this time more possessively. "You're not mine anymore."

On screen, he unhooked the ropes around my wrist. Here with me, he dragged the locator to a further point, where he fucked me from behind in this very bed with his hand on my throat.

Kind of... like the dream I had.

"How much?" I breathed out the words, clutching the sheet.

"A million euros."

No.

A sting spread in my heart. I felt like something shattered in me. Suddenly, his kisses hurt. His touch felt sore.

"You're not mine anymore," he breathed again, his fingers pushing my panties aside, coiling the string as he cupped my slick lips, covered in him.

He asked me in a whisper if I'd like to stop; his palm ground me harder. Pain sank in, but I shook my head.

He told me there was no camera around us when I took him in again. The stretch made me gasp, but I didn't care.

He wrapped his arms around me as I rode him in reverse, my knees pressed together, my chest full of emotions I couldn't voice.

I sobbed with my mouth shut, trembling every time he reached deep inside me.

"Why are you fucking me so hard, pretty girl?" he moaned out, his palms holding my tits as I slammed down on him in an act of self-destruction.

"You sold me..." I whispered; my nose felt sore.

"So this is revenge?"

"No..."

His hips twitched, his breath halted.

He caught my chin and turned my face to him. His eyes tensed, then he seized my lips. I moaned into his mouth as a pulse rose dangerously in my core.

He felt it too.

He grabbed me and lifted me off his lap, and before another word could be said, he threw me to the bed, lifted my legs, and shoved his cock back inside. He held me there and fucked my pussy hard and raw.

The bed cracked and shook.

My moans turned into cries.

I shouted when I came, my body bent and stiff. I was red hot in the head with my veins throbbing when he took his cock out and grunted. He shoved it deep inside me and locked me in the eye as he poured every drop inside me.

Then he caught my jaw with his hand and kissed me even harder.

"I lied," he whispered into my mouth, his hips twitching, still filling me up. "I got you."

He grinned on my lips, lingering just long enough to taste my reaction.

"The million was true, though. I turned it down."

He sat up and got dressed, and went out, leaving me... stunned.

I was still sitting in the exact same spot, staring blankly at the stain we left on the sheet when he came back. He fed me a cup of water and pressed a pill between my lips.

I swallowed it like a good girl, looking at him.

My head was ringing. My heart was still haunted by every single emotion that had shattered and trembled past me.

"What is it?" I murmured after a while.

"Birth control."

"Oh..."

He bit his lip sexily, pressing a kiss on my cheek. "No, it wasn't. Just a pain med with some delicious side effects."

My eyes flickered. My chest was again filled with a mixture of emotions I didn't know how to describe.

[ANNIEWALKERS88]: that pill is so worth it
[CRYBABY2345]: you should all thank me for taking off the blindfold. She's pretty.
[ANONYMOUSMEMBER23]: just took a shower with her. A close shot of her feet? — 20
[ANONYMOUSMEMBER011]: wanna see my girl bred again.
[ANONYMOUSMEMBER011]: half a mil?
[ANNIEWALKERS88]: make it a group effort. Happy to chime in.
[CRYBABY2345]: I'm sending in a woolie in next time

...

I had to assume that the camera stayed on 24/7. I had to assume everything that came out of his lips would be a lie.

Should I ask him what happened to the other girls?

Should I ask him how many girls there were before me? How many he was taking care of besides me?

I didn't know. I didn't know. All I knew was that whatever pill he gave me made me so horny that after he was gone, I got myself in the shower and pointed the showerhead at my pussy until I trembled in heat, crying.

Even then, the ache still demanded more.

Yeah, it was probably around the third time I fucked myself in the shower when I realized the camera was still rolling.

In here, the lights stayed on.

In here, time felt different.

I wished I had a watch, so I'd know for sure how long he had left me here.

But I hated myself for thinking like that, because I knew I didn't want a watch to tell time for myself. I wanted a watch so I could see how long he was out...

I felt insane.

I felt it crawling under my skin that I wanted him. Not just to kiss me and fuck me the way he did... I wanted him all to myself.

And I started to picture him saying the same thing he had said to me to another girl, fucking her pussy as hard as he fucked mine, and I started to get this really suffocated feeling in my chest, like I would hurt myself just to get his attention, while the root of my legs became slick and uncomfortable once again.

The room felt really small.

The dress was too tight.

I squeezed my legs and ground against the sheet. Somehow, I kept thinking about the blindfold and ropes, but I didn't dare take the dress off, at least not at first.

I felt slightly scared when I tore it, but it was a fleeting thought. I was too occupied with another to think it through.

I tore it into strips, wrapped one around my head, using it as a blindfold. Then I tied my hands to the head of the bed.

I knew they were watching me, and I knew when they saw that, they'd alert him, and whatever he was doing, he'd have to stop and come check on me.

I lay in bed, counting the numbers.

I counted to thirty when I heard him open the door. And my heart dropped back into my stomach.

He was right outside, which meant he wasn't in a recording session with another girl.

04:59:55

[ANNIEWALKERS88]: aint she a surprise
[CRYBABY2345]: horny girl wanted to be
tied up again
[ANONYMOUSMEMBER22]: bred by the gang.
Anyone? 50
[ANONYMOUSMEMBER011]: count me in - 30
[CRYBABY2345]: hell yeah!
[SYSTEM NOTICE]: 7 HOURS REMAINING.
[ANONYMOUSMEMBER044]: bring in the big
guns.

...

"You're fucking crazy."

He tore the blindfold I had made off my head and forced me to look him in the eye.

His fingers tightened on my chin so much that it hurt.

He stared down at me with such intention in his eyes. His shoulders rose up and down, but for a while, he didn't say a single word.

I bit my lip, staring back at him. My gaze fell to his lips.

He hit the table next to me, and it was so loud that a small scream slipped out of me.

I was so hard for him that even his anger turned me on.

I felt the mattress sink beside me as he climbed into bed with me. He pulled my blindfold down.

Darkness returned.

I tasted his lips on me.

It was an angry kiss, rough, painful, and messy. He shoved his tongue in my mouth and bit my lip until it bled, and the way I responded... I moaned so hard, like a kitten in heat.

Flushed, out of breath, with my legs wrapped around his waist, I ground against his crotch needily over his pants, making him fuck me fully clothed.

My fingernails dug into his back.

He sucked on my neck, and it felt like a punishment.

He bit my shoulder, thudding into my pussy over the fabric.

And I hopelessly soaked through the layers.

I was working myself up to the image of him coming into his pants, and he was daring me to take the pain.

Neither of us backed down.

It didn't take long for me to come, pussy clutching his cock over the fabric, and at the height of my orgasm, I started to feel a little bit of mental clarity — but only for a brief moment.

He unzipped and shoved his cock deep inside me, and I was a mess again. He came, spraying my womb, leaving me marked. I felt every single one of his twitches. In my pussy. And I still wanted more.

He licked the place he had bruised and was ready to put his cock back inside his pants, but I pinned him with my legs and thrust my hips.

My heart shattered when he tore the fabric I had wrapped around my wrists off, and then the blindfold I had made. Then he pressed his hands on mine and led them over my head. There, he fucked me with our fingers locked, our eyes staring into each other, full of the darkest impulses, until the drug wore off and I started to feel pain.

He fucked me a little longer, watching as pain spread in my eyes. He zipped up his pants and stood up after it was done. He gave me another pill.

I shook my head, refusing to take it.

"I don't like the side effects." I looked away. "It's making me think about crazy things."

"Like what?"

"Like you keep another girl in the next room, and when you're gone, you're with her," I blurted out, and regretted it immediately.

He curled his fingers, weighing the pill in his hand. Then he put it back on the nightstand and reached into his pocket. He took out a little bag and picked a different one. This time, he didn't ask me. He just pressed it between my lips and held a glass of water to my face.

I swallowed it, staring back at him as he watched me.

"Do you?"

He frowned.

"Keep a girl in the next room."

"Yes," he said coldly, placing the glass on the nightstand.

"Do you fuck her too?"

"Yes."

"On camera?"

"Yes."

I felt a sting in my mouth and pressed my lips together.

"And you like it?" I murmured, looking down at my fingers.

He ignored me and picked up the gag, pressing it into a ball. He stuffed it back into my mouth, ending this conversation.

I bit on the fabric instead of throwing it out, and for a while, I just sat at the edge of the bed, looking at him.

I didn't expect him to answer any of those questions, but he did, and there, I had what I had wanted to know.

I didn't understand why I had expected a different result.

I didn't understand why there was this big blob of sadness in my chest.

Just that I did.

"You asked the wrong questions, pretty girl," his voice softened a little, but was still cold. "What you should think about is how this will end for you."

"I'll die?" I spat out the gag. "Being sold to Annie-Walkers88? Or being pimped out? Yeah, I kind of expected that."

"Good."

And that was all he said.

He held his hand out, and I spat the gag into it, staring up at him. He closed his palm and headed to the door.

I watched him step out and close the door behind him. All I could think about was him heading into another room just like mine and kissing that girl the same way he'd kissed me before...

I had an impulse to stop him, but I didn't.

[ANNIEWALKERS88]: that was delicious.
[CRYBABY2345]: the lying or the girl?
[ANONYMOUSMEMBER044]: now I wish I was her first lol 50 — still wanna see her with the gang.
[ANONYMOUSMEMBER011]: second that, but put them in the same room, get her drunk, see if she'll bang the gang — 70
[CRYBABY2345]: 40 says she will
[ANNIEWALKERS88]: 60 says she won't
[ANONYMOUSMEMBER212]: 80 we make him tell her the truth.

...

A different drug.

A different effect.

The same me. Still replaying the image of him fucking a new girl, all tied up, in front of his cameras, his cock buried in her pussy, and her crying and moaning at the same time.

I was both aroused and terrified by that image because not long ago, I was that girl. His pretty girl. But I could never be his girl again because...

I wasn't the same anymore.

Not a scared little virgin.

Tied up.

Inexperienced.

He changed me.

And I let him.

I curled my legs and held them close to my chest.

Did I really care?

Did I really feel that insecure?

Was it just the drug or me?

I didn't know.

I didn't know.

Time felt like sandpaper grinding on my heart when he wasn't here. In a corner, I waited for his return — until the door was pushed open.

He held two bottles of cheap whiskey.

He came straight to me. His hand seized my chin and forced my mouth to open. I refused, so he kissed me until my jaw no longer fought against him. Then he poured the entire bottle down my throat.

I choked.

The liquid burned its way down, but it wasn't the pain that felt the sharpest. He held me in place and drained the bottle. I stared at him, with tears swirling in my eyes, hating him, resenting the fact that he was enjoying torturing me. By the time he emptied it, I was covered in liquor, gasping for air and coughing.

He dropped the other one on the nightstand, startling me with the loud thud.

"You want me to feed you again?" he asked coldly. "Or would you prefer to do it yourself?"

I glared back at him, remaining silent, not doing a damn thing.

He grabbed the bottle and twisted the cap open. He raised his hand and chugged half of it, then he pulled me to him and pressed his lips on mine. The liquid that had been in his mouth was now in mine, and he didn't even wait until I swallowed before deepening it into a kiss.

He continued drinking from the bottle and feeding

me with his mouth, then turning it into a kiss. I was drunk, dizzy, and breathless. My body was warm. He gripped me by the shoulder and kept feeding me until the bottle was empty, and I kept melting into his touch...

At some point, he smashed the empty bottle and laughed.

And there was this uncomfortable pressure in my stomach. I cramped and threw up everything that had been forced down my throat. His laughter sounded even more deranged next to me, but he held my hair and patted my back. When I was done hurling, he pulled me up and stamped a kiss on my lips.

I felt him grinning, and the next thing I knew, he tugged a bubblegum onto my tongue, biting me playfully.

I chewed it, not sure how I felt...

I hated him so much a few seconds ago, and now, I wanted to throw myself on him once again, and the thought made my nose a little sore.

"I need you to do something for me," he said, his fingertip brushing my shoulder. "It's very important to me."

I pouted, looking at him.

"I have this kink some may find... unconventional," he whispered. "I want to watch you fucked by a gang."

I widened my eyes, and my heart raced in my chest.

"It's such a turn-on for me," he said, biting his lip briefly. He turned to reach the pill from the nightstand, but instead of giving it to me, he pressed it to his tongue and let me watch him swallow. Then he took another one and held it between his teeth, like an invitation to the darker side of him. His hand reached behind my head and pressed me to him, and he watched me part my lips willingly.

"That's my girl." His eyes danced on my lips as I swallowed, and he watched me as the effects kicked in, faster this time because of the whiskey.

He snapped his fingers, and five guys appeared at the door. All wearing nothing but jeans, with their faces painted like his. They pulled me up and away from him, leading me to the bed, touching me, but my eyes lingered on him. He stood by the nightstand, his hand pressed to his crotch, eyes tense and much darker.

A pair of hands bent me to stay on all fours on the bed. A kind of dread seized my heart, and it almost made me want to beg him to stop this madness, but it left me before I could catch it.

The man behind me rubbed my wet pussy, still covered in him. Two others folded my nipples into their lips, rubbing their erections on me.

I moaned.

A moment of quietness later, I felt myself being slammed against a hot body.

I gasped.

My fingers clutched the edge of the bed. My eyes remained locked on him, and his dark, deep eyes were troubled by something dangerous and uncontainable inside. He walked to me, his hand falling to my neck, and there, he held my throat as I looked up at him. His cock was so hard in his pants that it looked like it would break the fabric. But he didn't take it out. He pulled my lower lip down with his thumb and fit it into my mouth, and in the loud sound of a man fucking my pussy from behind, he just gazed at me, his thumb tugging my tongue.

Moans spilled from my chest. I bounced harder on the guy's cock, sucking him and looking at him as he watched me.

I groaned like a little slut. My face was flushed, and my eyes were half-closed, but he locked me in the eye, refusing to let me close them.

The two other guys pulled me to sit up. They guided my hands to their cocks, and I stroked them as the guy behind me picked up his pace.

At that, his eyes tensed. He unzipped his pants slowly and held his cock to my face. The tip was already dripping, but he made it seem like it didn't matter at all.

I stuck my tongue out and licked it, then opened wide and took the whole thing in my mouth. His hand fell on the back of my head. Gently, he placed it there, letting me suck him and lick him while he watched.

I didn't quite understand what happened from that point on.

Just that another took over after the first guy finished on my back. I was positioned on someone's lap while another fucked my mouth.

He had me in his hand the whole time.

While every single place of mine became shared and owned.

My lips. My tits. My pussy. My ass.

There wasn't a place on me left untouched.

But all I felt was him.

His touch on my skin.

His gaze telling me I was doing a good job.

I felt feral.

I was in a daze.

The more I wanted him, the harder I fucked those guys until it was just the two of us. He had a camera in his hands and pointed the lens at me. He pressed a button to snap a shot, then moved to another angle. My cunt, my bruised legs, my chest covered in cum shots, my face still wet.

He made sure every angle was covered, then he put down the camera.

"Did you come?" he asked, his voice sinister and dangerous. I felt his fingers touching the side of my thighs softly, so soft as if I'd break at any second.

"Many times." I looked up at him, pressing my lips together. My throat was sore, and my mouth tasted like the last guy. But I didn't care. It was my turn at last, and I wanted him.

He smiled, but it was a cold one.

And he laughed, loud, with his whole body shaking, his voice torn — but for some reason it sounded hollow before it was sad.

He picked me up and took me to the bathroom. He turned on the water faucet and pushed me under the water, then rubbed shampoo into my hair and body wash onto my body.

At some point, he took off his belt and put it around my eyes, then kissed me under the water as the water washed the paint off his face. Then he pressed me against the wall and entered me. He kissed me while he fucked me, and I started to taste like him again. My body begged me to stop, but I told it to shut up.

"I saw you lusting after me the whole time," he whispered, trembling inside me.

"Call me *pretty girl* again," I begged, my pussy pulsing with pain.

Everything hurt, but I felt suffocated without it.

"Pretty girl," he murmured in my ear, his teeth brushing my earlobe.

I didn't really want to come again, but I wanted him.

"They get to share you, but they don't have the authority to breed you." He caught my wrists and pulled them over my head.

"Mine, mine, and mine..." he said as he pressed a kiss on my forehead, my eyes, and my nose.

I bit my lip, trying to suppress the way my body reacted to his words.

A good fifteen minutes later, my pussy spasmed, forcefully and painfully, as he made my lips bleed.

09:00:03

[SYSTEM NOTICE]: 3 HOURS REMAINING.

[CRYBABY2345]: that was a beautiful gang bang.

[ANNIEWALKERS88]: our girl didn't disappoint.

[ANONYMOUSMEMBER22]: @therealhost can we start bidding on how this end?

[ANNIEWALKERS88]: @therealhost I want her — 1 mil

[NOCALLERID404]: MINE. 5 MIL

[CRYBABY2345]: bullies! Anyone else want to make sure she stays with the livestream? - 80

[ANONYMOUSMEMBER011]: she stays - 90

[ANONYMOUSMEMBER444]: been saving for this. The girl stays — 3 mil

[ANNIEWALKERS88]: 7 mil.

[ANONYMOUSMEMBER22]: she   stays —
6 mil.

...

09:45:12

I had a feeling that this would end soon.

My first clue was when he put another red dress on me, tied my wrists in ropes again, and covered my eyes with a blindfold.

My second clue was when he took me back to the room that smelled like death and decay and pulled my wrists up to a hook.

I was back where I'd first started.

And this time, he grabbed a chair and sat down.

The camera never paused.

Everything that had happened between us, all that had been done to me, was a show...

People placing bids.

Him executing it.

Was any of it real?

I didn't know.

I didn't want to think about it because every time my

mind tried to go there, my nose started to get sore, and I didn't want to cry in this room again.

"What happens to me now?" I asked him, trying to distract myself.

I didn't expect him to answer, but he did.

"It always ends the same way," he said softly. He sounded a little tired. "Throat torn open. Wrists slit. Blah blah blah... But you know what's funny? Every time, they spend an hour throwing millions against each other, stupidly thinking one of them will have the girl. One against the world."

"You are the world?" I snorted.

"No!" he raised his voice. "The idea of a girl going home to any one of them is a betrayal to the others, so when one attempts to alter her fate, he becomes the enemy."

Right...

That actually makes sense.

"How much?" I didn't know why I was so calm, but I asked anyway.

"Usually around fifty mil."

"That's..." I wanted to say "a lot," but then—was that really how much my life was worth?

It took a village to kill a girl, and that village would only spend fifty mil to make that happen.

Suddenly, I didn't know what to think anymore.

"So you're a serial killer," I concluded. "Who funds your crime by going viral? Doesn't that take away from the kill?"

"Yes and no." He sounded smug.

"Have you placed a bid on me?"

"I did."

"To own me? Or to kill me?" I bit my lips.

"Isn't that the same?"

I could hear him laughing at me through the words, and he wasn't wrong.

I must be crazy to even think he'd want me alive.

He wanted to be the one to kill me.

It had always been his endgame.

This was his design.

His livestream.

His chatroom.

His crime...

I was just a pretty girl in his collection.

No name.

I started to wiggle my wrists again, even though they were covered in bruises and cuts.

"This is getting boring," he said after a while, stretching his arms.

I heard his bones crackling, and there was that light-hearted joy in his voice.

Then I heard him press a button, and the way his voice turned dark and sinister told me the break was over.

"As usual, the bidding doesn't end until eleven. I'll be back at that exact time for the grand reveal."

At that, he clicked the button again to mute the livestream.

The sound of his chair squeaking against the floor echoed as he stood up.

Then I heard his footsteps heading to the door.

"Please... don't leave me here," I begged.

I rolled my eyes at my own brain, still thinking about him going off to fuck another girl.

"Gotta go sharpen my knife, sweet girl," he chuckled, tapping on the wall.

And the door closed.

I was left there all on my own.

Soaked in the terror of my fate.

My ultimate death.

To become his, forever.

I thought about begging AnnieWalkers88 to outbid the others, but then I remembered he had turned off the mic.

And then I started to worry that if AnnieWalkers88 outbid the others, I'd be shipped off to some sick, wealthy man's mansion, chained in a cage until the day I died.

A caged bird.

Or his pretty girl?

It saddened me that part of me actually wanted to stay his, and what bothered me the most wasn't that I was going to die, but the fact that I was just one of many.

Tomorrow.

Next week.

Next month.

He'd whisper the same thing to another girl—looking like me, tasting like me, trembling like me.

And if I couldn't have him, then remember me.

It was then that I made my peace.

11:00:01

[SYSTEM NOTICE]: 1 HOUR REMAINING.

[SYSTEM NOTICE]: HOST RE-ENTERS THE LIVECHAT.

[CRYBABY2345]: yes, baby!

[SYSTEM NOTICE]: *ANNIEWALKERS88 HAS EXITED THE ROOM.*

[ANONYMOUSMEMBER22]: come on, now!!! cut this one slow and bloody.

[NOCALLERID404]: her finger — 11 mil

[CRYBABY2345]: make her beg first — 5

[ANONYMOUSMEMBER444]: her eyes — 5 mil

...

11:01:34

I heard the door open again.

His footsteps, awfully cheerful.

"How's my girl doing?" he asked. Even his voice sounded light and devilish. "Ready to be gutted?"

I kept my mouth shut, my chin up. My body shivered, not that I could control it.

This will all be over soon,

I told myself.

Everyone dies.

No big deal.

This will be over soon.

Tears rolled down my cheeks like beads falling off a necklace. I had no control over them either, but if I were in charge, I'd make it stop.

I heard him walk to me.

And a very cold thing touched my belly.

A blade.

He dragged it across my waist, and then I felt a sharp pain rising on my skin.

I gasped, loud, my body shaking hard.

He stopped in front of me, and I felt his hand reach my back, his palm warming me, and somehow, I started breathing again.

He stepped forward, and his breath spilled on my face.

"Shhh..." he hushed lovingly. "Don't be so scared. It's just going to hurt a little."

He nibbled on my nose as he dragged the blade up the side of my body. It tipped my chin to him, and I felt his grin on my lips, and the blade moved.

It brushed all the way up my arm.

There, he pressed me to his chest and carved something onto my wrist while he kissed away my tears.

I was supposed to be afraid. But all I felt was this odd comfort of being held by him.

That bastard.

I pressed my knees together.

Then he let me go.

"Let this be a reminder," he said slowly.

I didn't know if he was speaking to me or the crowd.

"I am your host," he stated, with an unchallengeable dominance in his voice. "Not a pet. This is my livestream. My game. My crime. I let you in on a little treat. You may participate and even bid on what I'll do to her next, but don't you ever forget what you are — my guests. This is what happens when you forget your manners."

I felt his hand leave me.

And the buzzing sounds of the machines started to fade.

And in seconds, the world was quiet.

Just him, breathing, in front of me.

He was still hard.

And I was still... bleeding.

He grabbed the blindfold off me, but before I could see a thing, he covered my eyes with his hand and pressed his lips on my neck.

He bit me softly, sucking on my skin hard as he dropped the knife on the floor.

And he didn't let me go until my arousal made my legs shiver.

"Those guys really pissed me off," he said, smearing the red across my neck. "It was time to teach them a lesson. Can't have them win every time."

"You're keeping me?" I bit my lip, too scared to let my heart sing.

"It seems like it."

He tugged on the ropes and let me down from the hook.

My arms fell on his shoulders.

"Can I be your only girl?" I blurted out.

"No," he rejected me. "And you better hope none of them survive the way you did."

"Can I bid?"

"With my money?"

I nodded, tensing up again.

"What a naughty girl."

He kept my lower lip between his teeth as he bit it playfully.

"Tell me, what's your bid gonna be?"

"That no one else makes it out alive," I said, as a mix of jealousy and dark intention raged inside my body like he had impregnated me with his evil seed.

My pussy clutched; a rush of neediness rose in my lower belly.

He moaned at my words, his eyes sparkling with something even darker.

"Good girl," he said. "Keep it up, and one of these days, I'll let you kill it."

And there, he smiled, big and wide.

He pressed a smack on my cheek, and the hand covering my eyes was lifted.

I opened my eyes, hoping to see him at last, but all I saw was him walking away from me.

On my arm, the stinging pain reminded me of what he had done.

I looked up.

And on it, it read,

"Pretty Girl. Mine."

"You coming with me?" his voice came from the dark corridor, the sound of his heels echoing in the hall.

I followed him to another room, looking almost identical to the one I'd been in.

There, he wrapped a rope around my throat and tightened it until I couldn't breathe.

And it was just me staring back at him with soulless eyes, watching him fall to the ground in an empty room, holding my motionless body, breaking down like the same little boy who had lost the one person who mattered most...

[SYSTEM NOTICE]: ALL ARCHIVABLE CONTENT DESTROYED. NO FINAL BID RECORDED.

THE END UNTIL IT'S NOT

from the author...

If you enjoyed this book, be a good girl and leave me a review.

If you hated this book, let others know!

Sign up for my newsletter to get notified about sequels, discounts, unfiltered editions, bonus chapters, and more exclusive content: https://www.thepunkhead.com/book-signup-form

continue reading...

His Winter Baby

On her way home for the holidays, Casey's car breaks down. With a storm closing in, she takes a ride from a stranger... In a cabin deep in the mountains where no one can hear her scream, he ties her to a bed and breeds her until spring comes. (HEA)

Spice level: 🔥🔥🔥🔥

My Latex Obsession

Saved by a serial killer, she becomes part of his doll collection, and he starts a nighttime routine. (HEA)

Spice level: 🔥🔥🔥🔥

No One But Her

A cop turns a case into a personal obsession in the shape of a cabin, a cage, and four walls of toys built just for her.

His Brother's Widow

After her husband's death, she seeks comfort in his twin and uncovers a shameful secret that's been part of her marriage from the start.

Theirs To Breed

On a cabin vacation with her best friend and his dad, she ends up in bed with them both.

A Priest's Good Girl

She comes to confess—he trains her to be his temple.

Stalk

She tries to get away, but he follows her to a new town, vowing to eliminate everything that stands between them.

coming next... santa's to do list

The Sneak Peek

ONCE UPON A TIME, *there was a girl who fell in love with a man. He took her virginity on the day she turned 19 and tied her to a chair, and she had been fucked ever since.*

That man was my stepfather, and that night was Christmas Eve. I was born on December 24, and every year, my family celebrated my birthday the same way they celebrated Christmas – with a house full of relatives, secret Santas, mistletoe, and eggnog. My stepfather would always dress up as Santa, and I would wear a red dress and striped socks to be Santa's girl.

Except this year, I had slutty lingerie underneath my innocent Christmas dress. I found it under my stepmother's pillow earlier today, where he had discreetly tucked it last night.

My lips? They were the rich, berry red he liked. And when I went into the room to blow out the candle, I caught him pressing his hand to his crotch with a bit of desperation and guilt, as if he had been thinking about my mouth blowing something else.

I wouldn't blame him.

You wouldn't either if you knew what I did.

I had been a naughty girl this year.

...

Pre-order on my website: https://www.thepunkhead. com/ebooks/

Amazon: Santa's To Do List by Katrina Yang